Dear Parent:
Your child's love of reading starts here!

Every child learns to read in a different way and at his or her own speed. Some go back and forth between reading levels and read favorite books again and again. Others read through each level in order. You can help your young reader improve and become more confident by encouraging his or her own interests and abilities. From books your child reads with you to the first books he or she reads alone, there are I Can Read Books for every stage of reading:

SHARED READING
Basic language, word repetition, and whimsical illustrations, ideal for sharing with your emergent reader

BEGINNING READING
Short sentences, familiar words, and simple concepts for children eager to read on their own

READING WITH HELP
Engaging stories, longer sentences, and language play for developing readers

READING ALONE
Complex plots, challenging vocabulary, and high-interest topics for the independent reader

ADVANCED READING
Short paragraphs, chapters, and exciting themes for the perfect bridge to chapter books

I Can Read Books have introduced children to the joy of reading since 1957. Featuring award-winning authors and illustrators and a fabulous cast of beloved characters, I Can Read Books set the standard for beginning readers.

A lifetime of discovery begins with the magical words "I Can Read!"

Visit www.icanread.com for information
on enriching your child's reading experience.

I Can Read Book® is a trademark of HarperCollins Publishers.

Plants vs. Zombies: Save Your Brains!
Text and illustrations © 2014 by Electronic Arts, Inc.
Plants vs. Zombies is a trademark of Electronic Arts Inc.
All rights reserved. Manufactured the U.S.A. No part of this book may be used or reproduced in any manner whatsoever without writ-
ten permission except in the case of brief quotations embodied in critical articles and reviews. For information address HarperCollins
Children's Books, a division of HarperCollins Publishers, 195 Broadway, New York, NY 10007.
www.icanread.com

Library of Congress catalog card number: 2013950295
ISBN 978-0-06-229496-8
Book Design by Victor Joseph Ochoa

19 20   CWM   25 24 23 22 21 20   ❖   First Edition

I Can Read!

READING WITH HELP 2

PLANTS vs. ZOMBIES

SAVE YOUR BRAINS!

By Catherine Hapka

HARPER
An Imprint of HarperCollinsPublishers

Hi there.

I'm Crazy Dave.

But you can

call me Crazy Dave.

I'm here to warn you that

the zombies are coming!

And they want to eat your brains!

You'll need to defend

your house and stop them.

So let's get to work!

The best way to stop

the zombies is with plants.

Yes, really!

Different plants stop

different zombies.

You'll need lots of plants
because there are lots of zombies
coming right now!

To keep all your plants healthy,
you'll need some Sunflowers.
Hurry up and plant some!
Sunflowers will help your garden
grow faster during the day.

When night falls, you need plants that don't need much sun.
Good thing there are plenty of mushrooms to choose from!

Oh no, here come more zombies!
Zombies aren't too bright.
But some of them have found
ways to protect themselves.
Some wear cones on their heads
and others wear buckets.

Some zombies use
different things as shields.
Newspapers and screen doors
are just two examples.

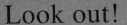

Look out!

I see a zombie waving a flag.

That means a huge wave

of zombies is coming.

I hope you're ready for them.

Because if you're not,

you can kiss your brains good-bye!

One thing about zombies:
they have been around
for a long time.

My time machine, Penny,
lets me travel back
to different places
in time.

In Egypt, there are
mummies and explorers.
Watch out for that
wave of Mummy Zombies!

In the Pirate Seas,
you'll need to beware
of Pirate Zombies.
And in the Wild West,
Cowboy Zombies
are all around.

Are you scared yet?

Don't worry! Just head

to my shop, Twiddydinkies.

It might not look very fancy.

But it has all the stuff you need

to keep the zombies

far away from your brains.

Remember, some plants take a while
to charge up.
Potato Mines should be
planted ahead of time.

But if you need to act right away,

know your peas!

Peashooter, Repeater,

Pea Pod, and Threepeater

make a good defense.

If you're in for a
wave of Pirate Zombies,
Snapdragon puts up
a fiery defense.

Bonk Choy packs a punch
that can defend against
Mummy Zombies
from all sides.

Uh-oh, now your brains
are really in trouble.
The zombies have made it
onto your roof!

Quick, grab some Flower Pots.

Then you can fight the zombies

with any of your plants.

Watch out for
the Catapult Zombie!
His basketballs
will flatten your plants.

You should plant an Umbrella Leaf.

It protects your plants

from catapults.

It also blocks Bungee Zombies.

They attack from above and

take your plants.

Look out!

Here comes Gargantuar.

He's the biggest zombie yet!

Try your own catapults
on this guy.
Use plants that toss
cabbages, corn, or melons.

Whew!

We fought them off this time.

Your brains are safe for now.

But the zombies will be back,

or my name's not Crazy Dave!